Ethan Long

PRESENTS

VALENSTEINS

(A LOVE STORY)

BLOOMSBURY
NEW YORK LONDON OXFORD NEW DELHI SYDNEY

First published in the United States of America in December 2017 by Bloomsbury Children's Books
www.bloomsbury.com

Bloomsbury is a registered trademark of Bloomsbury Publishing Plc

For information about permission to reproduce selections from this book, write to Permissions, Bloomsbury Children's Books, 1385 Broadway, New York, New York 10018
Bloomsbury books may be purchased for business or promotional use. For information on bulk purchases please contact Macmillan Corporate and Premium Sales Department at
specialmarkets@macmillan.com

Library of Congress Cataloging-in-Publication Data
available upon request
ISBN 978-1-61963-433-6 (hardcover) • ISBN 978-1-61963-435-0 (e-book) • ISBN 978-1-68119-664-0 (e-PDF)

Art created with graphite pencil on Strathmore drawing paper, then scanned and colorized digitally
Book design by Ethan Long and Yelena Safronova • Handlettering by Ethan Long; typeset in Sprocket BT
Printed in China by Leo Paper Products, Heshan, Guangdong
2 4 6 8 10 9 7 5 3 1

All papers used by Bloomsbury Publishing, Inc., are natural, recyclable products made from wood grown in well-managed forests. The manufacturing processes conform to the environmental regulations of the country of origin.

For my step mummy and real deady

It was a cold, dark night, perfect for scaring,
but Fran had something else on his mind.

Of course, Vladimir HAD to know what Fran was up to.

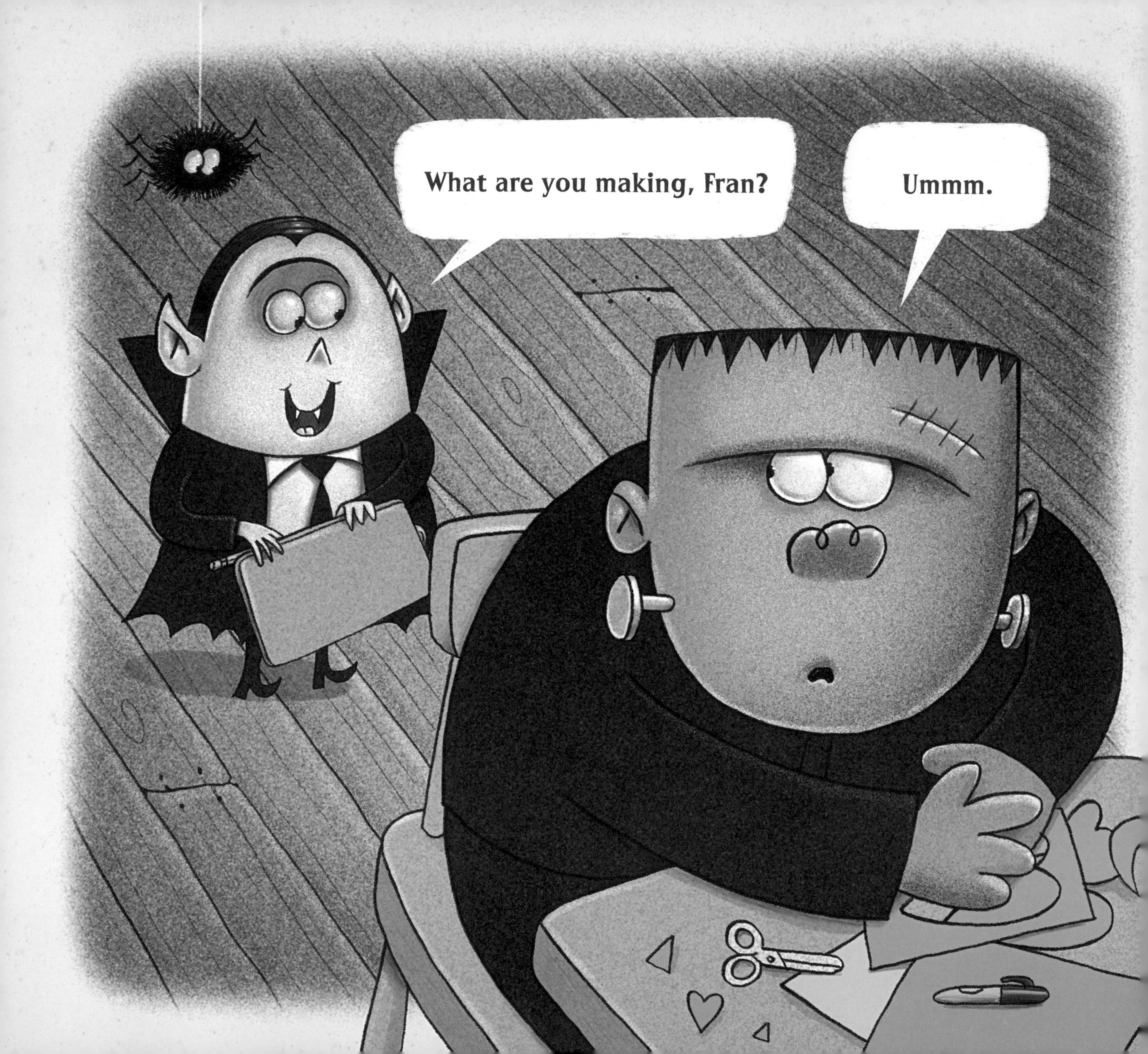
What are you making, Fran?
Ummm.

Bunny knew what was going on.

This is a heart, everyone! When you love someone, you cut one of these out and give it to them on Valentine's Day!

Sandy checked the calendar.

I'm never falling in love!
Love is so . . . YUCKY!
Not just yucky! It's TERRIFYING!

So he went outside to get some fresh air.

And that's when he was reminded that love isn't about
being mushy mushy or fluttering your eyes
or kissing someone on the lips . . .

. . . and it certainly isn't about cutting out paper hearts.

It's about something you feel in your *real* heart,
even if it does feel a little funny sometimes.